Please visit our website, www.garethstevens.com. For a free color catalog of all our high-quality books, call toll free 1-800-542-2595 or fax 1-877-542-2596.

Cataloging-in-Publication Data

Names: Crispin, Sam.
Title: Vomit! / Sam Crispin.
Description: New York : Gareth Stevens Publishing, 2018. | Series: Your body at its grossest | Includes index.
Identifiers: ISBN 9781482464801 (pbk.) | ISBN 9781482464825 (library bound) | ISBN 9781482464818 (6 pack)
Subjects: LCSH: Nausea–Juvenile literature. | Vomiting–Juvenile literature.
Classification: LCC RB150.N38 C75 2018 | DDC 616.047–dc23

Published in 2018 by
Gareth Stevens Publishing
111 East 14th Street, Suite 349
New York, NY 10003

Copyright © 2018 Gareth Stevens Publishing

Designer: Sarah Liddell
Editor: Ryan Nagelhout

Photo credits: Cover, p. 1 Jan H Andersen/Shutterstock.com; background gradient used throughout rubikscubefreak/Shutterstock.com; background bubbles used throughout ISebyl/Shutterstock.com; p. 5 maxim ibragimov/Shutterstock.com; p. 7 Africa Studio/Shutterstock.com; pp. 9, 11 chombosan/Shutterstock.com; p. 13 PHILIPIMAGE/Shutterstock.com; p. 15 sunabesyou/Shutterstock.com; p. 17 Photographee.eu/Shutterstock.com; p. 19 JPC-PROD/Shutterstock.com; p. 21 TinnaPong/Shutterstock.com.

All rights reserved. No part of this book may be reproduced in any form without permission in writing from the publisher, except by a reviewer.

Printed in China

CPSIA compliance information: Batch #CS17GS: For further information contact Gareth Stevens, New York, New York at 1-800-542-2595.

CONTENTS

Coming Up Again 4
What Do You Call It? 6
Down the Pipe 8
Something's Wrong 10
Why the Yuck? 12
Worried and Unbalanced 14
All Different Colors. 16
Mean Green 18
Take Care 20
Glossary. 22
For More Information. 23
Index 24

Boldface words appear in the glossary.

Coming Up Again

Throwing up is a part of life. You probably hate it. You might even be afraid of it. But there are as many reasons for throwing up as there are names for it. Let's learn more about vomit!

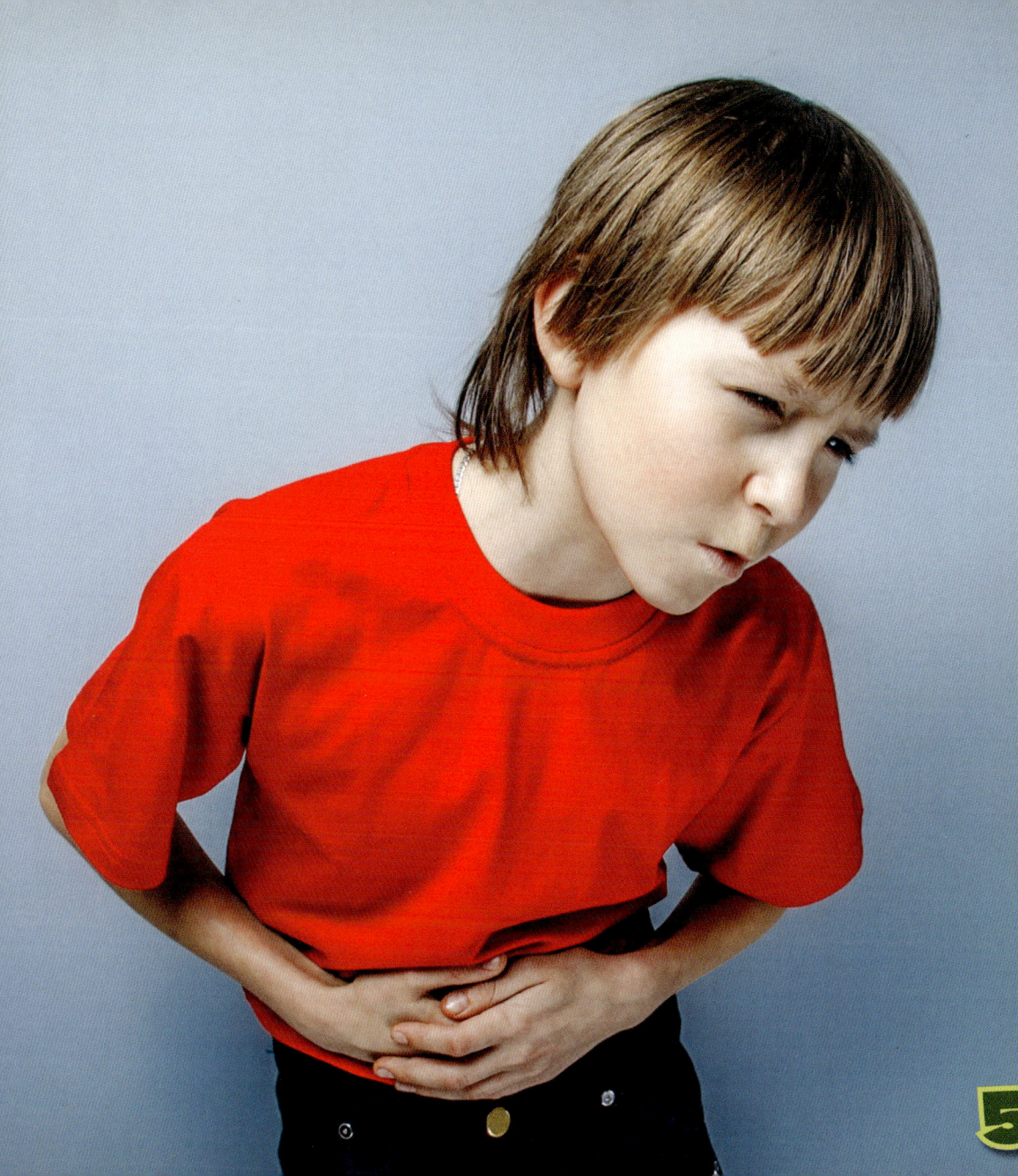

What Do You Call It?

"Vomiting" is the name doctors use for throwing up. It's the emptying by force of the food and other things in your stomach—through your mouth! There are lots of different words for vomit. Which one do you use?

OTHER NAMES FOR VOMIT

- SPEW
- HURL
- HEAVE
- THROW UP
- UPCHUCK
- SPIT UP
- PUKE
- BARF

Down the Pipe

When you eat, food travels through your digestive system. It goes down a tube called the esophagus (uh-SAH-fuh-guhs). It leads to your stomach. There, liquids break down the food before it moves to your **intestines**. When you're healthy, everything works perfectly!

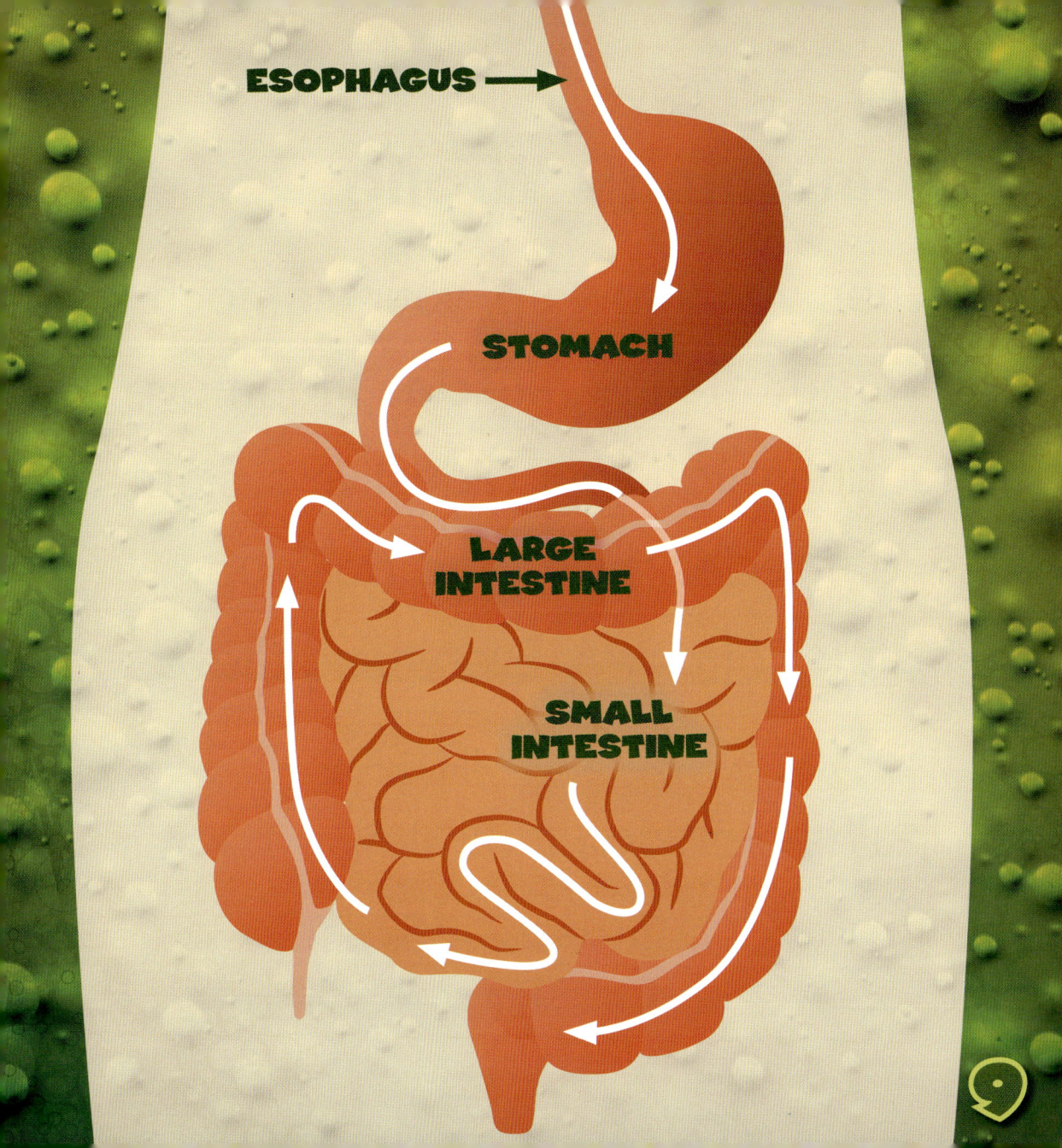

Why the Yuck?

There are lots of reasons you throw up. Most times, it's because you're sick. If you have a virus or **germs** in your stomach, your body tries to get rid of them by throwing up. You could also be nervous about something. Or you might puke if you spin around a lot and get **dizzy**!

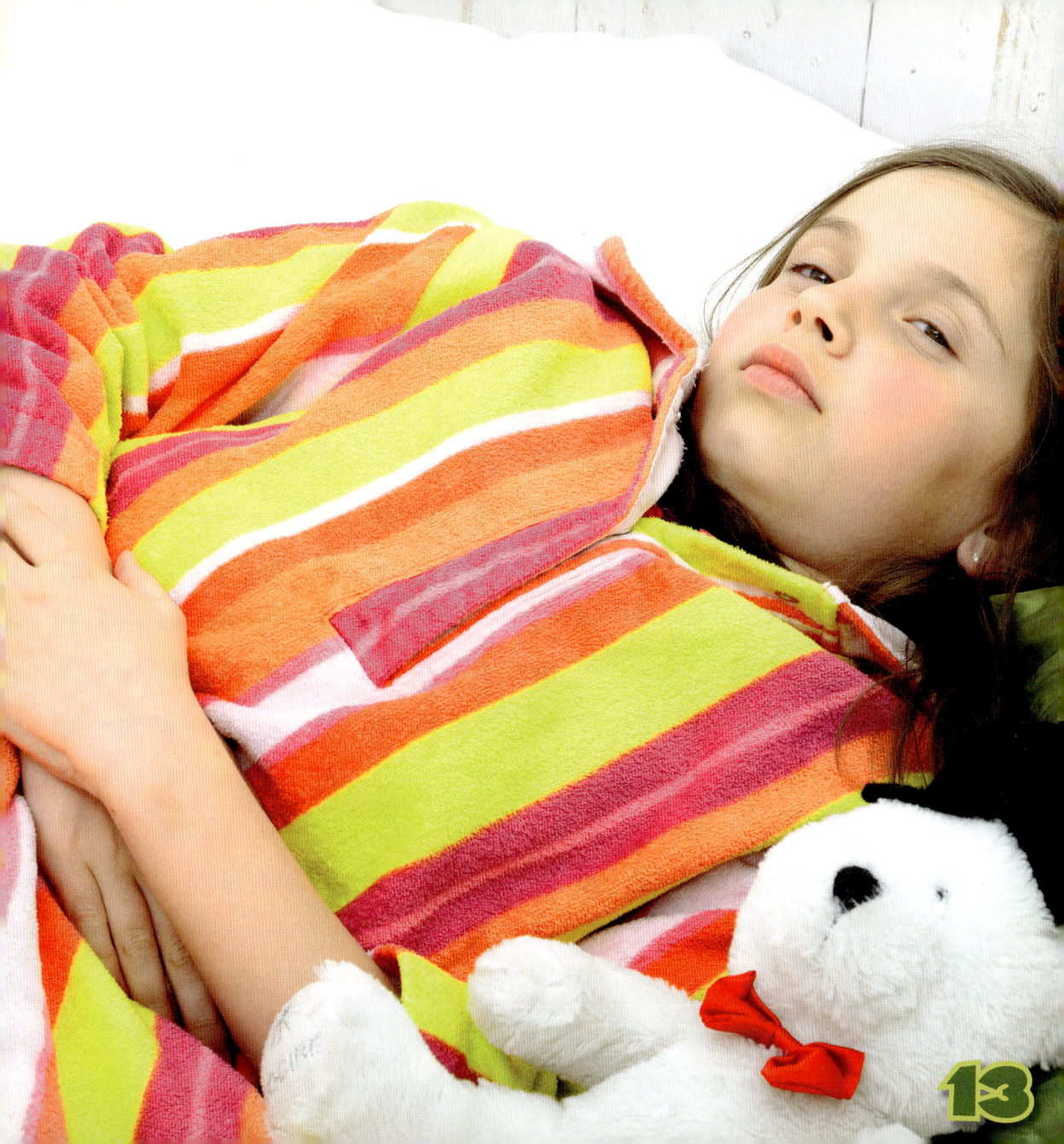

Worried and Unbalanced

Sometimes **stress** can cause you to throw up. So can certain **medicines** and **parasites**. Even your ears can make you throw up! Parts in your ears control your sense of balance. If it gets messed up, you might vomit!

REASONS YOU SPEW!

- LOSING SENSE OF BALANCE
- STRESS
- SICK
- PARASITES
- MEDICATION
- ATE SOMETHING BAD
- MOTION SICKNESS

All Different Colors

Vomit can be all sorts of colors and **textures**. It depends on what you ate. It's also different based on how recently you ate. If you throw up soon after eating, your puke might look like what you just ate!

Mean Green

If your barf is green, for example, it might have bile (BYL) in it. Bile is something that helps your intestines turn food into poop. If your puke is green, you're throwing up things from your intestines, too. You might need to see a doctor!

Take Care

When you throw up, you lose a lot of water in your body. Make sure to drink water afterwards so you don't get **dehydrated**. Throwing up is a sign something's off in your body. You have to take care of yourself!

GLOSSARY

dehydrate: to lose water or body fluids

dizzy: having a feeling of spinning

germ: a tiny living thing that can cause sickness

intestine: a long tube in the body that helps break down food after it leaves the stomach

medicine: a drug taken to make a sick person well

muscle: one of the parts of the body that allows movement

parasite: a living thing that lives in, on, or with another living thing and often harms it

stress: a state of concern, worry, or feeling nervous

texture: how something feels to touch

FOR MORE INFORMATION

BOOKS

Conrad, David. *Burps, Boogers, and Other Body Functions.* Mankato, MN: Capstone Press, 2012.

Miller, Connie Colwell. *The Pukey Book of Vomit.* Mankato, MN: Capstone Press, 2010.

WEBSITES

Adventures in Vomiting
webmd.com/children/features/adventures-in-vomiting#1
Read this to find out why we vomit.

Vomiting
kidshealth.org/en/parents/vomit.html
Learn more about what you should do if you vomit here.

What's Puke?
kidshealth.org/en/kids/puke.html
Find out more about vomit here.

Publisher's note to educators and parents: Our editors have carefully reviewed these websites to ensure that they are suitable for students. Many websites change frequently, however, and we cannot guarantee that a site's future contents will continue to meet our high standards of quality and educational value. Be advised that students should be closely supervised whenever they access the Internet.

INDEX

barf 7, 18
bile 18
colors 16
digestive system 8, 10
ears 14
esophagus 8
germs 12
intestines 8, 18
medicines 14, 15
mouth 6
muscles 10
parasites 14, 15
puke 7, 12, 16, 18
sense of balance 14, 15
stomach 6, 8, 10, 12
stress 14, 15
textures 16
throwing up 4, 6, 7, 12, 20
virus 12
water 20